For Sam, Anna, and Claire. I love you!

- Dad

Psalm 139:14

For Kari and Parker.

- Wes

www.mascotbooks.com

For more information, please contact:
Mascot Books
560 Herndon Parkway
Herndon, VA 20170
info@mascotbooks.com

CPSIA Code: PRT0515A
ISBN-13: 978-1-63177-215-3
Library of Congress Control Number: 2015906270
Printed in the United States

Yesterday it was my turn to bring something to class for show and tell.

I brought my
older brother,
Ryan!

When Ryan was born, his left hand was missing.
He learned to do everything anybody else could do, though.
He just did it a little bit differently.

When my friends saw Ryan, some of them said funny things, like:

I didn't care, and neither did Ryan. We're used to people not knowing what to say. If they found a $100 bill in a bag of potato chips, they would make the same sounds. His arm was a surprise, that's all.

My friends had a lot of questions for my brother.

Sam, who was the **tallest kid** in class, asked:

"Yep!" said Ryan. He showed us how he tied his shoes and said, "See? I can do it. I just do it a little bit differently."

Anna, who had **curly blonde hair,** asked:

CAN YOU RIDE A BIKE?

"Sure can!" said Ryan.
"I love riding my bike.
Especially going fast over jumps!"

Joey, who had **red hair,** asked:

CAN YOU
PLAY
BASEBALL?

"You bet!" said Ryan. "My favorite position is pitcher and one time I even hit a home run!"

Claire, who had a **birthmark** on her cheek, asked:

Noah, who **wore glasses**, asked:

CAN YOU JUMP ROPE?

June, who was the **shortest** kid in class, had been sitting off to the side. She quietly asked:

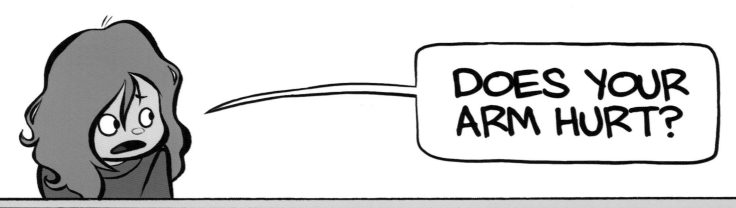

"Actually, no," said Ryan.

"Since I was born this way, it feels like any other part of my body. There's nothing to be afraid of."

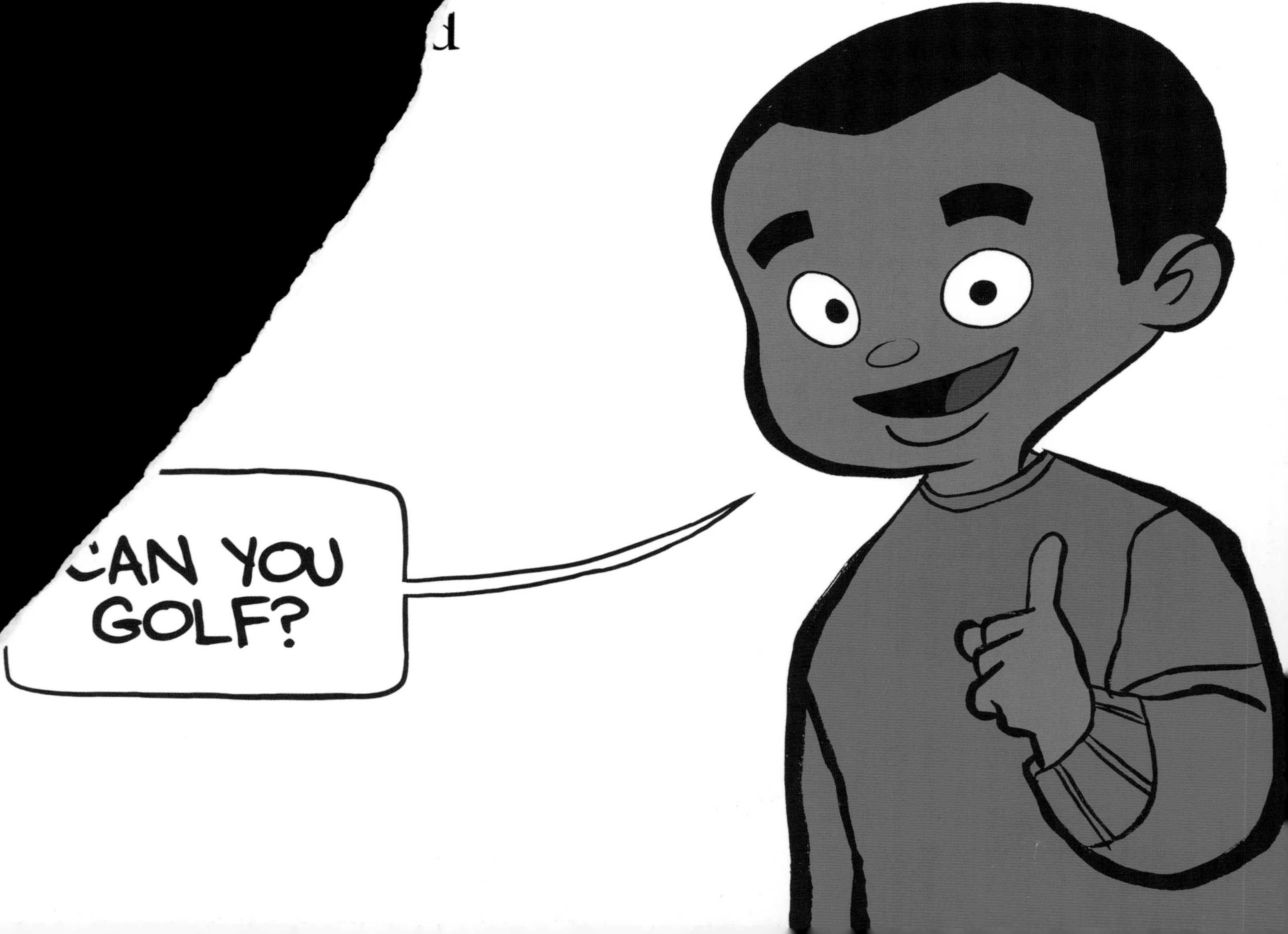

"For sure! I can hit the ball far and straight!"

Martin, who had a **cast on his leg,** asked:

CAN YOU PLAY VIDEO GAMES?

I was glad my brother came to show and tell.
He looks a little different than most of us, but
we're all different somehow, aren't we?

Jack had **green eyes** and Charlie had **dark skin**.
Martin had a **cast** and Billy was
missing his two front teeth. And me?
I have **freckles**.

Everyone is **different**,
and do you know what I think?

Being
different is
AWESOME!

What makes **you** awesome?

First of all, thank you to each and every Kickstarter backer who literally helped to make this dream become a reality! Couldn't have done this without you and am eternally grateful! I'm especially thankful for the support from my kids' school, Country View Elementary. Thank you, also, to my family and friends who helped me through this whole crazy process of bringing a book into the world. Thanks to Wes for bringing the story to life with his colorful, incredible illustrations. Thanks to Josh and everyone at Mascot Books for being excited about the project and making it happen.

Special thanks to my wife, Julie - Your patience with me is beyond understanding, but I'm grateful for it. Thank you for loving me no matter what and for believing in me even when it's hard to do so myself. You inspire me to keep growing, to keep loving, and to keep serving. Love you so much, Jules.

Dad - I know how proud you were of this project and I wish you were here to see it. I'd give anything for you to be able to read it to Sam, Anna and Claire, even just once. Thank you for supporting me, for loving me and Julie and the kids, and for the example you set. I miss you every day, but I know you're smiling. Love you.

- Ryan

Thanks to Ryan for inviting me to join him on this project; I'm very proud of what we created together and I know it will bless a lot of people! Thanks to Kari for being my biggest cheerleader, and for being ever so patient with me while I was working on the illustrations for this book. Thanks to Parker for being the coolest little kid in the entire universe!

- Wes

Ryan Haack is an author, a speaker, and the creator of LivingOneHanded.com. *Different Is Awesome!* is his first picture book and is based on a true story - his brother, Joey, brought him for show-and-tell! Ryan lives in southern Wisconsin with his wife, Julie, and his three awesome kids, Sam, Anna and Claire.

Wes Molebash is a freelance cartoonist and illustrator whose work has been featured in newspapers, books, websites, and magazines. He lives in Southern Ohio with his wife, Kari, and their son, Parker.

I'd love to hear and see how *Different Is Awesome!* has impacted you, your family and your school! Visit www.DifferentIsAwesome.com to share pictures, stories and to find other resources that will help you see the value in everyone! Thanks!